Chronicles of Heart

Flairs and Glairs
Publication House

"Chronicles of Heart"

ISBN No: " 9789391302252"
1ˢᵗ Edition
Language – English and Hindi

Flairs and Glairs
Publication House
Regd. Under MSME Act.

Disclaimer

This is a work of fiction and solely represent the thoughts of the corresponding authors of the articles.
Our editors have tried their best to edit the content of all the authors and check the plagiarism.
All the write-ups in this book are unique and are only published in this book.
In case any plagiarism or error is found, only the author is responsible alone, and not the publisher or the Compilers.

Cover Designing and Book Formatting
Shubham Shah and Ishani Agarwal

Acknowledgment

Dear Almighty, thank you for blessing me with the power and zeal to be able to complete this Anthology.
Also, Thank You dear parents, for trusting in me, and letting me work whenever I wanted. My family is the one who supported me for what I am today.
When it comes to this, Anthology, I would like to start with Thanking the Co -Authors, without your help and support, I would have never been able to complete it.
Thank you all of you, for being there. Much Love to all of you. I am glad to see you all standing by me.

Co Author

Shubham Shah (Founder Flairs and Glairs)
Ishani Agarwal (Co-Founder Flairs and Glairs)
Shivangi Jaiswal (Compiler)
1. Dilip M. Bhise
2. Risha Gogoi
3. Ashim Das
4. Arkadeb Dutta
5. Shreyangshi Chakraborty
6. Salma Faujia Islam
7. Ayanav Purkayastha
8. Prem Chandrakant Lalwani
9. Ashtha Barnwal
10. Sneha Chakrabarty
11. Sheetal Yadav
12. Insha Afreen
13. Aman Raj
14. Divyadharshini R
15. Kalparaj Chakraborty
16. Fiza Mansoor
17. Meghna Verma
18. T. Priyadharshini
19. Dr Amitha P Mani
20. Deepti Srivastava
21. Arnab Das Gupta
22. Shelma Jayan
23. Sufaya Yousf
24. Srinjoy Mitra

Shubham Shah

(Founder - Flairs and Glairs)

Shubham Shah, an entrepreneur at "Flairs & Glairs" a brand with dynamics in events organizing and cultural educational pan INDIA, is a 26yrs old guy who recently has entered the digital platform of imprinting emotions. He has initiated with his own open mic platform to help budding poets and aspiring writers under his brand named as "Teekhe Zasbaaat"

He is a commerce graduate from the Bhagalpur City of Bihar. He states Writing has impersonated him since childhood and he has now been writing for over a decade!

Cooking, on the other hand, is his passion! He also mentions, trying out new things just tickles him!

When asked sir, Why SPICY EMOTIONS?

He smiled and added, "agar jasbaat teekhe na ho toh wo jasbaat kahan" Spices are all that blends! So do his words!

As a chef, he presents to you his dish! Hot and freshly served! Taste it! Feel it! Enjoy it! You can also find his writing in the Book "Teekhe Zasbaaat" and 50+ Co -authored anthologies. With his passion to explore opportunities across Platforms, he is working with keen dev otion and We wish him all the very best for his future ventures.

He is Featured in the International Magazine DeMode for his upcoming solo novel.

He is Approved by Ne8x for its Lit Fest, and is a Golden Star Awards 2020 Winner.

He is a India Book of Records Holder for his Anthology Satrang, and has the Grandmaster title by Asia Book of Records, for the same.

He has also been featured in Prabhat Khabar, Dainik Jagran, and a lot of other Newspapers in Bihar for his achievements.

He has been a proud co-author to

India Book Of Records (Title- Black)

World Book Of Records (Title -15 Wonders of Poetries)

India Book Of Records (Title - Aaina)

Vajra World Records Holder (Title - Gustakhi Maaf Hai)

High Range of Records Holder (Title - Gustakhi Maaf Hai)

Indian Book of Records

(Title - Road from Worst to Best)

Share your reviews on his

INSTAGRAM
@spicy_emotions
@shubham4shah
Or via email on
shubham2shah@gmail.com

To stay tuned to his work and opportunities follow his business Handles

INSTAGRAM   FACEBOOK   YOUTUBE

@flairsandglairs
@teekhezasbaaat

WEBSITE:
https://flairsandglairs.in/
https://flairsandglairs.com/

Ishani Agarwal

(Co-Founder- Flairs and Glairs)

Ishani Agarwal hails from the City of Joy, Kolkata.
She is the co -founder of her Community "Teekhe Zasbaaat" and Flairs and Glairs Publication.
Been a Compiler for 45+ Anthologies, she is in the process for more. Co-authored in 150+ Anthologies. She is a India Book of Records Holder, a Vajra World Records Holder, a High Range of Records Holder, an OMG Book of Records Holder, a Bravo Record holder, a Forever Star Book of World Records and an Indian Book of Records Holder.
Approved by Ne8x for its Lit Fest 2020, and Literary Icon 2020. Also a Golden Star Awards Winner 2020.
She has also been award ed with India Star Republic Award 2021, a part of She Awards by Awards Arc and Winner of Nari Samman 2021 by Literoma.

She is also selected as Best Achiever of the Year by AwardsArc and Most Challenging Compiler Award by Spectrum Awards.
She got her first solo Published,a solo Compilation consisting of first 750 contents of hers, titled "Hand That Burnt While Healing".

She has been featured by the National Magazine "Taree Zameen Par" with the title 'unstoppable'.
Also featured in the International Magazine DeMode for her upcoming solo novel, she is proud to write on social issues, and is happy with the love she is receiving.
Connect with her on Instagram: @Ishani_agarwal_quotes / @compilations_so_far

Shivangi Jaiswal
(Compiler)

Shivangi Jaiswal is a Content Writer from Kolkata. Executive Head at "Flairs & Glairs" brand with dynamics in events organizing and cultural educational pan INDIA. Organizer at "The Glittering Fables" Writing Community. She is a B. Com Honors graduate. Certified in Stocks & Short Selling as well as Certified in Digital Marketing Been a keen student, she has recently been Certified for learning Spanish Language.

She is an Indian Book of Record Holder.
Approved by Ne8x for its Lit Fest 2020 for the Author of the Year 2020 and the Real Hero's Title 2020. Also, a Warrior of Change Awardee 2021
She loves to bring smiles and happiness to many faces, so she is into Social service.
Traveler, Teacher, Meditator, Dancer, Singer, Instrument Player. She loves to play guitar and harmonium. Also been awarded in many events for winning many categories Been a Public Speaker she has taken part in many events and nailed it. Been a great Advisor to many. She has also been crowned for winning Miss Great Podium 2020 Tit   le in the category Modelling recently. Sports freak of Swimming and Badminton with a passion so strong. Since, past one year she has started her writing journey.
She writes so that many people can connect with their stories and get positive hopes. She thi nks " Every story is unique so embrace yourself to the best". She is a writer by day and a reader by night. Been a Complier of 3 2+ Anthologies, and in process for more, also Co - authored 1 20+ anthologies. Shivangi is an old soul with young eyes, a vintage heart, and a beautiful mind."

You can follow her work:
Instagram
@the_knockingvibe
@house_of_compilations

Whispers of True Mates.

Her penning flowed
like an ocean,
And came up the shore.

Underneath her diary,
The waves of her pain
was buried.

A storm rolled with each
line she wrote
Secrets in black ink on
white paper.
As she revealed her every
bit of piece.

The Diary listened to
her secrets.
The rolling of tears
dropped down,
and penned
several disasters.

And then she lay
deadly calm
On her dairy, as it was
her pillow,
who never scattered her pain,
Rather than giving
her a shoulder to lean.

No more Whispers of Pen

that night,
As she found her
True Mate Diary & Pen
That Night.

The Starry Night

The sky was full of stars,
So, lit
So beautiful,
by splendor of the moon.

Looking up in the sky,
I see your face.
Your passionate love
have made me sure.

Because in the garden
of my heart, you grew
a heart with your love.
Kissing my soul, and
making it heal.

The two great eyes slay,
and beauty struck a spark
between them.

Writing Miracle

Writing Miracle my love.
It happens, so wait, feel and jot down.
As many things work in mysterious ways.

Keeping focus and full patience
Let's play with words
And make a new destination.

Times seems to stop, and go slow.
A single line written on diary claims
That love is Arriving soon.

Collectable stories, poems of write-ups
Grows valuable as each passing day.

So, fall in love with inking.
The love which will make you fall into it
by each passing day.
Because the beauty of inking makes
you fall with your beauty.

Happiness Is Worthwhile.

Happiness is worthwhile.
Something that cannot be denied.

Something which will help you smile on dreary days.
Something that cheers your tones.

Something that helps you to choose,
to stay or move on.
Some try to steal it away, from each other.

But what is yours will stay with you forever.
Don't let anyone take it away from you something deep and
elegant.

You should always look within yourself.
Because smiles suit you.
And lives within you.

Dilip M. Bhise

Dilip M. Bhise is a Mumbai -based prolific short story writer and poet at heart. He has shared his writings in many anthologies of Writersvilla, Flairs & Glairs, Unvoiced Heart, Spot Write, And Wordsgenix Publications. His Seven anthologies as a co-author are already published:

1.   The short story 'SAM'S UNSPOKEN WORLD' in the book 'HEART BOATS' published by WRITERSVILLA publication

2.   The short story 'HARSH REALITY in the book GLIMPSE OF HARSH REALITY by FLAIRS AND GLAIRS publication

 3. Poetry collections ' Bond That Neve r Ends', Reminiscence by Writers Villa Publication

4. Poetry Collections 'Life', Nanhe Farishtey, Wings of Fancy by Flairs and Glairs publication, and many anthologies are awaited to air.

Presently Junior Lecturer, Department of English, G. D. Goenka International School, Surat, has been teaching (English language and literature) for over a decade. He is a Ph.D. scholar of Savitribai Phule Pune University, Pune Maharashtra, and writes fictional, non fictional stories, Haikus, and poetry, sensing where you are reading makes perfect sense. He loves to rhyme his mind and bask in the warmth of poetry which seems to be the elixir of life for him.

Tending

Nowhere! I am with me,
If not reminded being alive
Sometimes sleep seems evidently clearer to see
Dreams forgetting oneself for a while
Let me voice myself my friend
Let me step on the crackling disdain
Let me not just brag to be good to other hands
Let me go beyond my worldly affairs and mend
Mend that impenetrating walls between mortals
Mend that no means can have ever curtail
Mend that unfathomable depth of deadly behavioral trails
Mend that hosts of futility between good and evil
Evil which has stretched its hands
Not to hug you my friend but to offend
And keep no way left for moral errand
So, it's a high time to keep a closer eye and tend
Tend but not just to showcase or mere merry making
but tend to uncover brutal mind and conspiracy marching
Tend that intention where only material happiness comes first
and not human being
Tend to stitch that patch   of inequality and agonizing amoral
social setting

Pandemic Covid -19, A Dubious Phenomenon

Who's really benefitted at the act of COVID-19?
Is that the earth for its cleanness?
Or non -mammalian for stopping devastation of forest for a
while
Or ecosystem to breathe in newly
Or the enemy of unruly human beings to see stopped new
crimes
Or someone else from extraterrestrial bodies to attack and
conquer the earth?
Or a lesson seeker to follow rules of nature
Or an evil warmer to be contaminated and contaminate others
Or troubled one at the degradation of the lovely environment
to see mischief hands of
humans locked in the houses
Or a poverty-ridden to redeem meager help out of sympathy
Or a corruption driven to get relief seeing all offices
temporarily shut
Or a savior of this beautiful earth seeing locked up ever
destructive hand of a naughty
creature of this nature itself who is called human being??
Brains?
That's the question, if you know the answer let me know

Risha Gogoi

Born in Assam and brought up in Haryana, Miss Risha Gogoi is currently a medical student studying at Gauhati Medical College, Guwahati, Assam.
Poetry is one of those things that fascinates her. So, she tries to put her thoughts on the paper through her poems.

Broken

There they lay,
motionless and still –the broken pieces
Of humanity!
Some were sparkling like diamonds under the light,
While others imitated rubies,
that were bereaved of their shine
by jealous blood stains…

There she lay in a corner;
her shrunken self-confirming ease in the afterlife!
On the pillow of blood,
Her head rested,
Waiting for her scarf to absorb away
the dreams she was having!
Her lifeless cheeks blushed painfully,
with a hue fainter than her sindoor;
Both marking their bond with the man
she had once belonged to!
Her throat bore the daily voice of agony,
when he used to leave the essence of his fingers there –
Fingers that she wished to interpose with hers forever;
Fingers that had not hesitated to break the wine glass
and her dignity both at her face,
And fingers that proved his physical strength and rage
mightier than her love!

There she still lies,
amidst the intoxicated air,
waiting for the veil of darkness to lift!
And there they still lie –the broken pieces of glass,
that witnessed the darkness soar

Ashim Das

Ashim is a 21 -year-old boy. He's from a small town called Gauripur, with not so small dreams. He's currently   perusing Food Tech from BFIT Dehradun. He did his schooling from JNV Dhubri and his Higher Secondary from SPHS Dhubri. He's currently confused about where his life is taking him. He picks interest in most of the things around him and tries to do it. That makes him good in a lot of things but perfect in almost nothing. He writes poems, sings and even make songs of his own. He's devoted to   Music. He hopes to be acknowledged through these hobbies of his.

Regrets with My Dream

You came in like the breeze, this ruined my vacancy
I wished you'd let me stay, along with you for eternity;
I left my heart open, like an open door
But you came no more, although you knew the steps to my door.
My vibrating breaths found its way up to you,
With my cold feet, I ran through the crowded street;
I was beat, that doesn't mean I'd accept defeat
But it seemed that destiny didn't want us to meet.
Everyone went past, only I was left at last
In the crowded streets of vacancy.
A day came after a long bore, when I saw you on the shore
Alone in the dusk and dark I went, I guess it was all meant.
You were alone, speaking on your phone
I was glad, it was over after a moment
I wasn't the one you've been waiting for,
I wasn't the one you were wanting for,
It ravaged me, our fulfilment.
I saw you with someone else, in envy my heart melts
I couldn't wait there anymore, it broke my heart's core
My life was once again in a bore.
This is where our story ended in vain
But after that, a new love story began.

The Visual Perception

Arose in the mid of the dark hours
While the moon beams were striking me,
What's more captivating than a bouquet of flowers?
What on earth is deeper than the sea?
In the midst of the night, this notion struck my brain
The thing that's brighter than light,
Whose sight stops the blood in my veins.
All the answers let me to your eyes
Well, that's no ordinary thing,
Prettier than any other human being.
They are so tender, it lets my heart surrender
I still recall the first time our eyes met,
Our gazes parted too soon, we noticed each other grin
They are as calm as the moon, it's you I'd love to win.
Lost in your eyes, hard to bid you bye
Infinite like the stars that shine
All I want is you to be mine.

Arkadeb Dutta

Arkadeb Dutta born on 13th May, 2000, hailing from Kolkata, West Bengal is an author, poet and writer. He thought that pen is mightier than sword and a poem speaks more than voice. He penned down his thoughts in the form of poem and writings. He is a dreamer who believe everything which someone can dream he can achieve.

।। तुम ना मिले ।।

आज यादोंकि दराज़ खोली,
पुराने कुछ खत मिले,
खत में लिखि कुछ दिल के टुकडे मिले,
कुछ वादे मिले,
बरती मुलाकाते मिली,
उन बरते नोक-झोक के जवाब मिले,
बहौत तलाशा मगर तुम ना मिले।।
वक़्त के सिल्वटों में लिखि कुछ राते मिली,
तुम्हारी खुशबू मिली,
कुछ बदलते मौसम कि अल्फाज़ मिले,
तुम्हारे लिये लिखे कुछ शेर मिले,
टूटे फूटे अल्फाज़ मिले,
साथ देखे कुछ ख्वाब मिले,
बहौत तलाशा मगर तुम ना मिले।।

Shreyangshi Chakraborty

She is Shreyangshi Chakraborty, currently pursuing
her bachelor's degree in economics. In between
finance and statistics, she loves to rhyme poetries.
Being more of an introvert, she also finds herself
spending a lot of time painting.
She also has a soft corner for dance, so if she is not
writing, reading or painting, probably you will find her
dancing to her own rhythm.

Fall in Love

Fall in love with the happily ever after,
And the star lit lusters.
Fall in love with the lips that smile,
And the soul that is so versatile.
Fall in love with the purity of those eyes,
And the heart that want to feel the beautiful
paradise.
No, I am not telling you to be the damsel in distress,
Waiting for a prince to take you out of the mess.
Neither I am not telling you to believe in fairy tale
Nor to wait for the perfect ship to sail.
But sweetheart fall in love with the beauty of your
eyes,
And those lips that smile on the sight of pretty
fireflies.
Fall in love with your heart, soul and mind,
Maybe calm, maybe chaotic but it's all finely
designed.
Fall in love with the happiness that comes from
within,
You and only you are the reason for your beautiful
tale to begin.
If you have your prince is all good and fine,
But if you don't, you still do shine

Salma Faujia Islam

Salma F. Islam is a 19-year-old budding writer from Mangaldai, Darrang, Assam. She is pursuing Civil Engineering (B.Tech) from DBCET, Guwahati. Her hobbies include painting and writing. She believes "When we fall in love with our dreams, we rise."

Is She A Paradox??

She wants to fly, but she wants to gaze at the vibrant world
too;
She wants to run, but she wants to rest and sit too.
She is a grown up, but she possesses the Peter Pan Syndrome
too;
She is the sweetest girl, but she can be barbaric too.
She loves fiction, but she believes in entity too;
She loves to dream, but she keeps her pace in this engrossed
world too.
She proves herself to be bold, but she is sensitive too;
She tries to prove the existence of hopeless romantics, but
she does believe in fidelity too.
So, what should she be called now???
Is she a collection of paradoxes???

Destiny Is Handmade

"It's okay!! Your failure was anyway pre-destined."
Often spoken by oldies on our interim decline.
We awfully accept it despising our luck,
Without glimpsing on our blunder chuck.
We forget the need of our diligent work,
Just to allow people to mock.
We forget the need of our pious invocation,
Just to consider ourselves dereliction.
Can't we create our own destiny by our devotion?
Can't we create our own destiny by our
devotion?
Let's change the history;
Pick up the pen,
And write your own story.
Just for once, let's contemplate,
Destiny to be one's volition, not predestination.
Destiny to be handmade, not one's fate.

Ayanav Purkayastha

Ayanav Purkayastha is a boy from Udharbond a small village from Assam. He has completed his bachelor degree in commerce and is going under MA in English. He writes small stories, poems and also articles. He is presently serving as a teacher in his locality.

Bliss of Fortitude

One day moving too speedy
was in the hurry to get ready;
The inner struck me once
but the fastness makes it all bounce.
In hurry, moved to the way
to keep with time, got on the bay.
At last, bucked the destination,
all set for the presentation.
Nothing was in the hand
all efforts got end.
The guy was suffering
and it all keep me in remembering:
Whatever you could do, do it
It may be the best or the least".

Incredible Master

One day, in the sparkling sunshine
Moving to and fro along the vine
Attempts were made to get out
But every single time it created a doubt.

Being helpless, I stood there
From nowhere a scream appear
I stir my head over and over
Find a tiny sparrow in a cover.

The chirruping made me baffle
Neither way nor anything to snaffle
The tiny moved on the branches
Looking far way for any chances.

Soon it flew away in the blue
I was left without any clue
Few moments later it arrives
With a chance to survive.

The tiny made way with grain
In the pattern of a drain
Master to be needed indeed
The tiny made me freed.

(Teacher may be many, in many forms
Accept them without any norms
Live to survive, but for other
Teachers are the best example forever)

Prem Chandrakant Lalwani

Prem Lalwani, born on 26th July, 2001 is a MBBS student. Writing is one of the many hobbies he has. Born and brought up in Surat, he possesses a creative personality and believes that writing is a wonderful art and it can have a great impact on others. Moreover, he follows what he thinks that everyone is talented in some or the other way and one should never stop exploring one's own self!

To The Girl

Wish it was so easy to restrict myself from thinking about you as it is to you. Though it brings a lot of unsatisfaction but i guess the heart likes it. It has got so obsessed with you that it has lost the track of good and bad for itself. My heart has already made enough space for you that it has started forgetting its own existence. Heartfelt songs just pass by leaving a huge void, a void for nothing but a saddening realization of how badly it craves for you.

When Zakir Khan said that in a relationship we win once when it started and lose once when it ends. But we win and lose every single day in one sided love and I felt it. I win when you even rarely reply to my story, I win when I see that our choice of memes and posts matches, I win when I see you vibing on the same song I like, I win when youstill follow me (on IG) in spite of my shitty stories that I share. It maybe "just a thing" for others but I swear it's the actual motivation that never makes me give up on you.

But I lost today when I didn't even receive a birthday wish from you. Yet the biggest defeat: you aren't even reading this. But no matter what, its only me who rules this one sided - relationship which is as real as it is imaginary. You don't get to control it unless you actually participate. If I can live with this reality then i don't need any shadowing fantasies for my unapproachable survival requirements. I am happy with having dreamt, imagined and virtually lived every beautiful moment possible with you. Makes me so enchanted and euphoric. Though it would be no more than Deja vu for me when it turns real, though the novelty of moments might not thrill me as it may to you; but I'll bear with it since I love you so much.

Ashtha Barnwal

Ashtha Barnwal was born on 15th August 2000 in Bihar but later shifted to Vapi, Gujarat.
A Medical student full of energy and high spirit.
She is a cheerful and interactive person.
This is her first project as a writter.
Her philosophy is Life is short. Do what g ives you immense happiness

The Mask

For the world she could never keep a secret,
little did she know her life was itself one..
giving shoulders to cry on;
but never asked for one.
Do you know what she was the best at -
hiding those tears behind that dangling smile !

For the world she was an extrovert;
but deep inside only she knew her reality,
She was no less than an introvert covered with a tinge of
extravert.

For the world she used to be the calmest person ever,
but her reality splurted out only in front of a reflector..
She never knew how to be angry to the world,
but deep inside she was angry with herself..

For the world she was an amiable soul,
but little did she know that the most bubbly person was
actually the loneliest soul..

For the world she had a lot of friends,
but actually she was locked in a world of temporary people..
In the world of prioritisation,
she could never top someone's list..

Still she was cheerful;
happy from outside but with a question always,
"Will she ever be able to remove her mask?"
her answer was clear -
everyday in the morning she was ready with her mask on..
The question is still the same,
"Will that mask be ever demolished?"

Sneha Chakrabarty

Reader by passion, Reviewer by choice. I am a student of English Literature. Chocolate and books are my favorite companion. I have so much to share that paper seems to be the most patient listener.

Fearing the Unknown

When all of a sudden, she found herself confined in a dark room, she stood up, trying to figure out where she was and how she ended up there. It took her no time to   realize it was not a place she had been before. "Is someone here?" asked she. No one replied. There was nothing except silence. She could feel her heart skip faster. The last memory she has, is sitting in her room working on a laptop. She then hears footsteps heading towards the door she was captured at. Her heart beat started blistering. Suddenly the door opened and a little ray of light poured into the room. She could only comprehend a masculine figure by its shadow, his steps forwarding towards her, but couldn't recognize him out of the darkness. She ran towards the almirah and hid herself in the corner as she cou ld feel her nerves break down. Her heart pounded so hard that it could burst out at any moment.

While the silence was extreme, the only thing audible was his footsteps; which suddenly stopped. On not hearing the footsteps anymore, she came out of her hide feeling relieved. Instantly she felt a strong hand on her shoulder. The man behind slowly whispered in her ear, "I found you". He turned her and asked if she could remember him. She couldn't utter a single word as she was frozen with fear. Yes! It was him , the reason of her most traumatic experience in life. She had escaped from his clutches 4 years ago; shifted to a new place bearing new identity. She had never thought her past would ever strike her back.

He leaned on her and said, "Get ready to witness   the end sweetheart" and thrust the knife into her stomach. The act happened so sudden that she couldn't understand anything. All she could feel was the pain that the knife caused and pool of blood oozing down her. While she suffered in pain, he twisted

the knife with a bright smile on his face and enjoyed her suffering.

She strived really hard to survive when she heard a soft voice calling her name. Aadhya Aadhya, wake up or else you'll be late for office. She woke up to her nightmare. Oh! What a horrific nightmare it was she fussed. On a thought of it, she realized it just to be a mere nightmare foreseeing the past to knock her door in future.

Sheetal Yadav

Sheetal Yadav is an MBBS student, studying at Government Medical College, Surat. She wrote her first poem in 7th standard for a state level competition and had won 2nd prize in the competition. Since then, she has been writing poems and essays in Hindi and has won prizes at state and national level competitions. Through her poems she tries to portray the different shades of human character and emotions; as well as the societal problems.

<u>अय्याशी</u>

सतरंगी आसमाँ है,
महफ़िल मे आने लगी जान है।
होठों पर लाली है,
मदहोशी सी छाई है।
नैन मेरे कजरारे है,
इत्र से महकते मेरे अंग सारे हैं।

ढलने लगी ये शाम है,
तुम्हारे दीदार का इंतज़ार है;
फूट रहे हैं अंकुर अरमानो के,
तरस रहे हैं हम,
तुम्हारे नहीं आने से।

अब देरी का बहाना ना दो,
सर्द पड़े इस जिस्म में
थोड़ी- सी जान फूँक दो।
उँगलियों से ना जाम छलकाओ,
ज़रा उन्हें मुझ पर आज़माओ।
तुम्हारी नींद से ज़्यादा सुकून है मुझमें,
तुम्हारी जाम से ज़्यादा नशा।
डूबते चले जाओगे,
इतना गहरा है दिल मेरा।

खुद को अय्याश कहते हो,
पर, सारी दुनिया से आशिक की तरह लड़ते हो।
मुझको तवायफ बोलते हो,
अपना हाल- ऐ- दिल भी मुझे बयां करते हो।
अपने रंग से रंगकर मुझे,
क्यों अपनाने से इंकार करते हो?

Insha Afreen

Insha Afreen is a poet born in Patna,Bihar. She can be perfectly defined as a people person. She us a high   -spirited medical student and also shares a great interest in poetry. This is her first work as a poet. She believes that with the power of pen a person can bring great changes in the world.

Kuch Iss Tarah Si Mohabbat

"Humesha" bas kehne ke liye nhi,
Mera zindagi bhar saath de paoge kya?

Facebook, insta par humari photo post karne ki jagah,
Humare photo ki ek hardcopy apne wallet me rakh paoge
kya?

WhatsApp par regular conversation achcha hai,
Par roz mujhse phone par baat kar paoge kya?

Long drive, late night movies pasand hai mujhe,
Par roz mere liye kuch waqt nikaal paoge kya?

Yu toh mujhe khud ke liye bolna aata hai,
Par meri khamoshi ki awaaz ban paoge kya?

Khud se bhi zyada bharosa karti hu tum par,
Uss tarah hi tum mujh par bhi aitbaar kar paoge kya?

Parchaai bhi andheron me saath chhor deti hai,
Mera ta-umar saath de paoge kya?

Toh Bolo,
Mujhse ta-hayat mohabbat kar paoge kya?

Aman Raj

Here Aman Raj was born in Jamshedpur (Jharkhand) and raised in Banka (Bihar). He is a 2nd year medical student in Jaipur the (pink city of Rajasthan). He loves to study his favorite subject Biology and some motivational books. In his free time, he loves to draw, write all kind of writeup.

Anger the Worst Enemy.

We are all the slaves of our emotions. There are both negative and positive emotions that govern our mind positive emotions are those that bring happiness to us as well as to all those around us. These emotions are love, compassion, forgiveness and kindness etc. Negative emotions are those that make us restless and unhappy and also force us to spread the same to eve ryone around. Hate, envy, jealousy, possessiveness, suspicion etc are negative emotions anger however is perhaps the most destructive of all emotions. Anger is one emotion that change the person completely. Anger causecertain changes in the body - the blood begin to circulate faster; the eyes became red and some people even tremble with anger. When anger takes control of anyone it makes him violent, aggressive and unreasonable. The main problem is that the angry person refuses to listen to any sense and he continues to burn within. He may be vocal and start shouting. Some people throw anything that comes within their reach. They slam doors, kick thing abuse, curse, hit out, box and some even my when they are angry. Anger changes a man into an animal. The most sensible person can turn almost insane for the moment when he is ruled byanger. People say things that they regret later. They lose friends they hurt their families. It takes a lot of endurance from those who live with people with quick or hot tempers. Anger destroys one's peace of mind and the minute one sees it rising one must begin to breathe deeply or count to ten. This distracts the mind from the taught that cause the anger. Meditation and prayer are also good ways to control this extremely destructive emotions. People often make great mistakes in their lives when they are angry. They spend many year's in trying to undo the damage that they cause to other and most of all to themselves.

Happiness

Happiness is s omething which we can't describe in words it can only be felt from someone expression of a smile. Likewise, happiness is a signal or identification of good and prosperous life. Happiness is very simple to feel and difficult to describe. Moreover, happiness comes from within and no one can steal your happiness.

Q. can money buy you happiness?

Every day we see and meet people who look happy from the outside but deep down they are broken and are sad from the inside. For many people, money is the main cause ofhappiness or grief. But this is not right. Money can buy you food, luxurious house, healthy lifestyle, servants and many more facilities, but money can't buy you happiness. And if money can buy happiness, then the rich would be the happiest person on the earth. But we see a contrary image of the rich as they are sad, fearful, anxious, stressed and suffering from various problems. In addition, they have money still they lake in social life with their lack in social life with their family especially with their wives and this is the main cause of divorce among them. Also due to money, they feel insecurity that everyone is after their money so to safe guard their money and them they hire security. While the condition of the poor is just the opposite. They do not have money but they are happy with a stress free from these problems. In addition, they take care of their wife and children and their divorce rate is also very low.

Divyadharshini R

Divyadharshini R, an MA English and Bachelor of Education graduate. Born on 15th May, 1995 in Honnatty, Kotagiri, The Nilgiris. As a student in the past, planned to achieve more, yet possessed with obstacles. Now, mom to an angel. She took her to the path of success. Th ough she ten months old, her eyes motivate and says, "you can succeed."
An upcoming poet with intention of becoming successful one day.

Comfort Versus Suffer

Home life which alienated,
Not much life of polluted,
Things become demanded,
Forgot not to be remembered.

Home life which enjoyed,
Food and water possessed,
Movies which stalled,
Mattress knows weighed.

Life's not much easier,
People who roamed at road,
Food and water starved,
Child in hand and wept.

Not everyone's days are best,
Life is to be lived in peace,
Live your life with enough,
Think of people has none.

Kalparaj Chakraborty

Kalparaj is a teacher by profession. He completed his Master's Degree in English Literature from North - Eastern Hill University, Meghalaya. He also holds a number of other Diplomas from different institutions in India and abroad. These include Diplomas in Counseling, Psychotherapy, Psychiatry, Psychology and Journalism. He is a Graduate in Indian Classical Music, Bhatkhande Sangeet Vidyapith, Lucknow. He takes interest in reading, creative writing and music.

I Am 21st Century

I am 21st Century
Somewhere in the cosmos I dwell,
Words of Violence and hatred I spell,
Prayers and Worships, I abandon,
God and Divinity, I scorn,
Innocence I kill in charity
I am 21st Century.
Emotions I trample; Faith I plunder;
Humanity, I wrench asunder,
Jealousy, malevolence, communalism-I spread,
Dishonesty my blanket; Disloyalty my bed,
Corruption and Terrorism – Born out of me
I am 21st Century.
The only weapon I have is War.
Peace and Happiness, with IT, I mar,
Money and Power – My Sword and Shield
Out of these, brutality I yield.
But I am not any vicious entity.
I am the product of your Cruelty,
I Am 21st Century

Fiza Mansoor

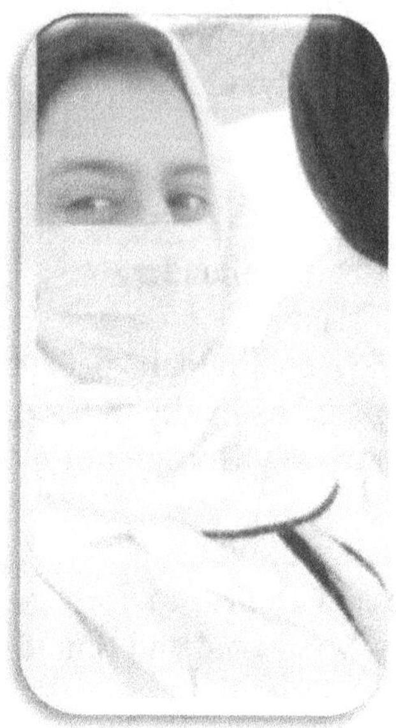

Fiza mansoor is a writer and medical student. She started her writing career with quotes. When she felt that people are giving their precious time to her   writings, they are reading them with passion, then she started writing poetry, stories and poems to continue. She started pouring her ideas on paper at the age of 17. Writing for her is a passion that she says that will never die. She believes that only writings can lighten a heart which is full of emotions.

Lockdown Musings

God tempted this race with an arduous ordeal which lingered
so long,
And I started listening to melancholy song,
Reminiscing all diem that we can't go out along,
Contemplating that if it will abide yearlong,
Will I dare to be throughout strong?
What this race did diurnal that coerce something vastly wrong,
Mouth sealed and enshrouded by a mask,
Don't know who cursed this race by praying for us this arduous
task,
I crave to ask,
This thing to my god standing calix to the oriel in bask,
Holding in my one hand a flagon and a brew flask,
Pondering when I will discard this hefty mask,
Observing the surge in the contagious cases,
Makes me sensed like I cannot visit other places,
Because this phage badly chases,
Which is well stamped on folks faces,
Who lost their cherished ones leaving on their hearts hurtful
and Unforgettable traces,
This phage honestly didn't ambushed folks on the premise of
races.

Meghna Verma

She is Meghna Verma. She is from Samastipur, Bihar. She loves writing. Her hobby is writing poetry, reading Novels and singing. She wishes to get name and fame in the field of poetry.

क्या कभी देखी है एकतरफा दोस्ती?

एकतरफा प्यार कि तो सब बातें करते हैं,
मगर क्या कभी देखी है एकतरफा दोस्ती?

कभी खुद पाने से ज्यादा किया है किसी के लिए?
खुद रो कर हंसाया है कभी दोस्तों को।
क्या किया है हजार बार माफ किसी को
क्या कभी देखी है एकतरफा दोस्ती?

क्या दि है कभी अहमियत सबसे ज्यादा दोस्तों को
क्या रोएं हो कभी दोस्तों के लिए भी?
क्या कभी देखी है एकतरफा दोस्ती?
खुद के गमों को भूलाकर,
क्या सुलझाई है परेशानी सब की?
क्या कभी देखी है एकतरफा दोस्ती?

हर पल खुद तन्हा होकर,
क्या हमदर्द बने हो किसी दूसरे के?
क्या हर दोस्त खोने के बाद भी,
रखा है एतबार दोस्ती पर ।
क्या कभी देखी है एकतरफा दोस्ती?
क्या कभी देखी है एकतरफा दोस्ती?

हां मुझे अकेले रहना पसंद है।

हां मुझे अकेले रहना पसंद है।
क्योंकि सब मुझे छोड़ जाते हैं।
सारे रिश्ते से मुंह मोड़ जाते हैं,
मुझे तोड़ जाते हैं।
कुछ पल में ही सब भूल जाते हैं,
खास से आम कर जाते हैं।
और फिर मैं बड़ी मुश्किल से खुद को संभालता हूं,
अपने आंसुओं को पोंछ कर खुद को खुद हि समझाता हूं।
दूर रहूंगा लोगों से,
न आने दूंगा किसी शख्स को जिंदगी में,
ये वादा खुद से करता हूं।

हां डरता हूं रिश्ते बनाने से,
किसी के करीब आने से
मगर फिर भी तुम्हें आने दिया था,
शायद जिंदगी कि कुछ सीख बाकी थी।
ठीक समझा था तुमने,
मुझे अकेले रहना पसंद है।
हां मुझे अकेले रहना पसंद है।

T. Priyadharshini

She's Priyadharshini. Mom's Princess. She's in love with English literature and so she loves to write blogs, poems, quotes and short stories. She's longing to etch her name in the world of remarkable authors. A budding writer and a movie lover too.

Melting Minutes of My Life

My fingers randomly turned the leaves of the book,
I just skimmed through the words of the page,
But I couldn't centralize my thoughts,
My mind was swirling around dreary ruminations,
I was utterly enervated out of striving,
My head was about to explode out of cretinous stress,
My state of efficiency has drained,
Tears rolled down and smudged the letters of the page.

Mom...
I missed her so badly,
All I need was her warmthful hug,
I coveted for her to wipe my hot tears,
I just wanted to sense her kiss on my forehead,
Interminable work load pressured her a lot,
Though she made time for me,
To console me, to uplift me, to vitalize me,
But it wasn't sufficient for me.

I want her to stay by my side,
Till I regain my energy,
I mumbled in my sombre voice to God,
"I need her the most at this time,
Please liberate her from her round-the-clock work schedule";
Think so may be my silent prayers were heard,
'Lockdown' may be a bane for many,
But for me it is a once in a lifetime boon.

Nine months, Nine whole months;
Indelible days of my life with my mom,
The days which I longed for,
The days which I ought to etch in my book of life,

The days where I relished each and every minute with my mom,
The days where I found absolute serenity,
The days which gave a unique world,
The world where we both   resided with sheer love and happiness.

The days which made me look so woebegone but also,
The days which diminished my crestfallen thoughts,
The days which made me to relinquish the idea of relinquishing,
The days which gave me back my mom's love, cuddles   and kisses,
The days which gave me ample of priceless minutes with my mom,
The golden days which I cannot get back in my hands thereafter,
The minutes which melted my heart but,
The minutes that I'll freeze it in my heart forever.

Dedicated to my mom.

Dr Amitha P Mani

Dr Amitha P Mani is a faculty member in the post graduate department of English at MES Asmabi College, P Vemballur, Kodungallur, Thrissur, Kerala. She is basically from Ernakulam district, but lives in Kodungallur with herhusband, son and parents. Her areas of interest include English Language Teaching, Narratology and Gender Studies.

Realizing the Basal: The Pandemic Impact

Though she was a firm believer, her concept of God was not acceptable to the family. It was a traditional Hindu family that performed routine temple visits, holy rites, usual chanting and fasting. For her evening is the time she got to work hard for her studies and do her daily chores. She was used to abstain from the evening temple visits as it spoiled her whole day. Can the loud reciting bring sanctity to soul or peace to the mind? For her, the perfect homework for the next day enabled her to work for a b etter tomorrow. One needs to be loyal to the customary practices in the family, otherwise the family muse would not stand with her at the time of crisis. For the rhetorical question, can anyone stand with one's inner self at any crucial juncture, the answer is an emphatic 'no.'

Self-help and appreciation are the best things one can do for inner peace; on the other hand, this will lead to genuine humane feelings discarding the mundane performances. At that time the lockdown was declared as an impact of Covd 19. With the other shutting downs, places of worship were also closed. That which was lost by the family members by not going for these regular visits was the darkness that covered the mind, though occasional visits turn out to be good to eliminate the negativity as believed by her. Thus, she got perfect opportunity to go back to her real self, read and understand a lot along with the family. The period taught that worship of God need not be displayed, but can be done in mind, for such people work itself is worship. She counted these among the very few benefits of the pandemic period.

Deepti Srivastava

Deepti Srivastava from Sonebhadra (UP). A very enthusiastic person. For her writing journey was started from lockdown . And now it has become a very amazing journey fir her. And this is not the end.

लॉक डाउन की कहानी

क्या हमने कभी 2020 के पहले लॉकडाउन या क्वॉरेंटाइन जैसे शब्दों का नाम सुना था जिंदगी की हकीकत से रूबरू कराया हमें 2020 ने। साल जब शुरू हुआ तो उसका भी स्वागत वैसे ही किया जैसे हर साल का करते हैं लेकिन जिंदगी को कुछ और ही मंजूर था । उस जंगल की आग में ना जाने कितने मासूम जानवर जल गए गलती किसकी थी यह बात किसी को नहीं पता पर सजा उन मासूमों को मिली । साल की शुरुआत कितनी भयावह हुई तो लगा मानो अब इससे बुरा भी कुछ हो सकता है पर यह तो बस शुरुआत थी असली मौत का मंजर तो अभी बाकी था।

होली के रंग अभी धोले भी नहीं थे कि एक विदेशी मेहमान के आने से हमारा पूरा देश कोरोना वायरस जैसी महामारी की चपेट में आ गया।उस वायरस ने जाति धर्म मजहब कुछ ना देखा सब को एक समान कष्ट दिए क्या अमीर क्या गरीब कौन जवान कौन बूढ़ा बच्चे तक को ना छोड़ा उसके चपेट में हर कोई आया। उस महामारी में हमने क्या कुछ ना देखा

अपनों से दूर हुए तो अपनों की कीमत पता चली
6 महीने जब घर में बंद हुए तब उन मासूम जानवरों की पीड़ा समझ आई।
अपनों से मिले भी हम दोबारा मोबाइल के अलावा भी दुनिया होती है. किसका भी एहसास हमें लॉकडाउन ने ही कराया था घरवालों के साथ रहना हंसी मजाक वह जो बचपन में खेलते थे वह दिन वापस से लौट आए थे हमारे।

जिंदगी एक जैसी नहीं होती कभी हार तो कभी जीत लगी रहती है उस मंजर ने भी हमें यह बताया और हम तो इंसान हैं मुश्किल वक्त में भी अच्छे पल ढूंढ ही लेते हैं.
है ना

Arnab Dasgupta

Arnab Dasgupta, an MBA and an IT professional working for IT & ITES Sales and Account Management Team.

He is a person with varied emotions running in his heart and mind. His words can show what emotions he has. He has a habit of penning down his thoughts, and currently discovering and exploring a hidden writer in himself. He has incorporated his study of spectrum of emotions in words. His writing and photography skills were published in several magazines, and he is also a co-author of several anthologies.

Hope you love the words and worlds.

Follow him on: Insta @imarnab_dg. Anyone can contact him on arnab-dasgupta@hotmail.com

Humanity Has No Lockdown

It was close to 10 o'clock in the morning. The DND flyover (Delhi–Noida Direct Flyway), an eight-laned 9.2 km (5.7 mi) long access-controlled expressway which connects Delhi to Noida was desolated.

A bike in full-speed was coming from Noida side was stopped at the Police checkpoint on the way to Delhi. It was near Mayur Vihar on the eastern side of the Yamuna river. There were blood stains on the rider's cloth, and also the rider was without a helmet.

It is illegal to drive a two-wheeler without a helmet. Normally, if a person is caught without a helmet his papers are checked, and he is immediately charged with a fine of Rs. 6   00 to Rs. 1000/-. Not only this, the officials of the Motor Vehicle Department can disqualify the driving license for three months. During lockdown the penalty could have been severe.

The on-duty police officers stopped the bike, asked the papers for the bike, wanted to know the reason for fast driving without helmet, and also the reason for blood stain on his clothes.

"Good Morning Sir. I am Bashir Beg coming from Sector 62, Noida. I am heading towards a blood bank near Akshardham to fetch a bottle of b lood for my 61 -year-old mother Raziya, who is suffering from thalassemia.

I was in a hurry of getting the blood as the blood bank does not have AB+ blood in their stock. Even being a universal blood recipient, nobody wants to donate blood to my mother. Even they were not ready to take my blood. The hospital member informed that I can get blood from a blood bank near Akshardham

In an urgency, I forgot to carry the helmet, and while I was near Sector 15, the wheel of the bike skidded. The blood stains are due to several cuts and bruises across my body.

However, I needed the blood at any cost. I picked up the bike and set off again without caring about the injury. Now, you have stopped me in order to check details." Bashir said.

After over-hearing the entire incident, another officer Naman Pandey came forward and asked Bashir to sit in the police jeep. He asked another officer, David to drive the bike, and follow the jeep.

Naman assured injured Bashir that he did not need to donate blood in this   condition, instead he would donate blood for Bashir's mother.

Upon hearing of Naman's decision, the on -duty officers immediately allowed him and David to go with Bashir.

Naman went to the blood bank near Akshardham, donated 'O Negative' blood (a universa l donor), and David also donated 'A positive' blood. In return, Bashir got two bottles of AB+ blood. Bashir returned to hospital along with Naman and David. He handed over the 'AB+' blood for his mother to the doctor. Naman ordered hospital to do a checkup and bandage for Bashir at entirely no-cost.

David returned the bike keys to Bashir, and both the officers left.

Shelma Jayan

Shelma Jayan was born on 23rd May 1992 in Trivandrum, Kerala. She is presently employed as a Postal Assistant and is married to Shri. J.S Jayasenan, a Scientific Assistant. She graduated with a Master's in English. Brought up in a family of educators, teaching is a pr   ofession that she has always revered. She is now in her journey to become a lecturer.

What She Taught Me?

Radiance of mornings have taught me...
That the little flowers in my lawn
Can lip on me and gently winks;
That the beautiful fish in my pot
Can flying over with her fins;
That the brownish beetles in my plot
Can sweetly sing in swaying winds.

Ambience of noons have taught me...
That the rays of sun and waves of sea
Are seeking for a secret space;
That the letters lying in my shelf
Are searching one to share her tales;
That the warmth of fear and cold of lust
Are sleeping in my charming dress.

Transcience of nights have taught me...
That the faded memories in my heart
Are getting shattered one fine day;
That the bunch of dreams I've treasured
Are being doleful another day;
That the precious person farther away
Is no more with me in this day.

Sufaya Yousf

Sufaya yousf is hailing from Kashmir India. she is currently persuing her bachelor's degree at Srinager kashmir. She is very passionate about writing poetry. She is a co   -author of more than 10 books. She is very hard worker and dedicated writer with positive attitude.

Happiness

Happiness is a precious necklace,
On the body of your life.
Smiles are priceless diamonds,
Today will become history,
While tomorrow is still a mystery,
Live your life, which is Now.
Because no one knows the tomorrow.
Be happy and make others happy too
This is the worship we all should do.
Serve the love, serve the care
Life is very short here.
Learn to love yourself and others too
You will get real happiness and peace too.
Smile, smile, as much you can
It reduces your and others pain.
Be a good person by heart
Life on earth too short.
Be in service of others
Give them hope in all matters.
Happiness is a precious necklace
So be wise to confess.

Buckle Up and Face the Challenges.

Buckle up and face the challenges of world
Don't think that you have failed and messed up,
You are more than what you just portray,
You have to run and hop,
And still, stand strong,
You have to find each day
with a conscious effort to find glee,
The mountains you walk on
get too steep to climb
Don't feel stuck in your life
Your Ambitions and goals still live
In the end, there is always a bright light
That you hold within
Look inside and light up the spark.

Srinjoy Mitra

Srinjoy is a 16 years old teenager reading in   Don Bosco School, Kolkata and is an avid reader. He is passionate about painting, writing articles, poems, short stories and play dialogues. He is also a keen   debater. He has received accolades in national and international level painting, writing and speech competitions . He is also learning German and recently received a scholarship for a trip to Germany in 2019.

The Hunt for The Hidden Treasure.

" Vallika , I have prepared your luncheon and have brought it here. Kindly relish it and take care of your health ", said Vijaylakshmi. Vallika Kutty was a senile woman who dwelt in the village of Nayarambalam, in southern Kochi. It was a magical village with a dr amatic seashore, thick forests and muscular peaks. Diminutive huts with creepers above it were scattered amidst Nayarambalam. Leaves fluttered and tossed in amazement.

Some coconut trees , which reached upto the sky were twisted hands, while some defoliate d trees were absolutely bony skeletons swaying in the breeze. Some juvenile village buddies really admired an old coconut tree, by the flank of the Periyar river , and recognised it as their tall   - sturdy friend. The Periyar river which passed through the   village , drained water , as cold as ice. Sometimes, a game of ' Kancha ' or ' Lagori ' was played among the children. The woman carried   water   in   decorative   pitchers   ,   from   the Kudumbadhree , a pond with water , as hot as a coal. This pond was at the south ern tip of the village , just behind the hut of Vallika Kutty.

All the villagers were contented. Vallika Kutty was an old villager and was also esteemed at by the kith   - and - kins, because her husband Yadavendra was at one time , the village sarpanch. But her health did not keep sound and deteriorated. At times , her neighbours Vijaylakshmi or Indumukhi would offer her meals, otherwise , she passed her days in terrible hunger.

One December evening , two teenagers , arrived at the village , and spoke to the sarpanch, Indumukhi 's husband , " Sir , we are from " The Photography Group of ' On am International School ' in Kochi . " They showed a few certificates and papers and were immediately escorted to one

of the huts which was vacant and uninhabited. For th   e next few weeks , Udayan and Ujjayini , the recent tourists remained busy beavers , clicking pictures, marvelling the many breathtaking sites of the village. They seemed delighted and hoped they would excel in their project. They climbed up tall coconut t   rees , drank their water and also played and spent time with the village children, seeming as mischievous as a marmoset, but they thoroughly enjoyed the trip.

The second week , when Monday mischief continued near the Kudumbashree pond and when they found t   he air extremely invigorating , Shardul, a village boy and son of Vijaylakshmi , on displaying a few perfect sites for photography , suddenly slipped and tumbled. Ujjayini found a lustrous stone , under the bushy side of the pond. " What a strange beauty !   Marvellous , "said Shardool, rubbing his back in pain. They found another diamond near Vallika 's hut. Without a second thought, they immediately approached the sarpanch and informed him about the matter.   " It's exceptionally priceless ! " cried the sarp anch. On conversing further with Indumukhi's mother   - in - law, who perhaps knew about Vallika's history, they could deduce everything.

" Yadavendra was the great   - grandson of Nadirvendra Shahzad; a born dacoit and leader of the ' Muruggan Gang ' , the fi ercest plunderers of that time in India. He had looted innumerable riches during the conquest of Hyder Ali in Kochi in 1773 , " informed his mother.

" Where are those affluences? " asked Udayan , rather inquisitive. All of them scampered to Vallika 's hut and began their search. " I think we need to dig deep here." These places have rough bumps " , said Ujjaiyini. As they dug and dug , to their astonishment, they discovered a tunnel filled with gold , emerald and diamonds. Antique idols of gods and goddesse s were also found. The tunnel had no end to wealth. The treasure was and would make one had his decendants

live a luxurious life. As the villagers heard about it , they created a pandemonium.

The goverment also payed homage and honour to Udayan and Ujjayini for their exploration. They gave twenty percent of the treasure as a reward to the kids and twenty percent of the treasure to the village of Nayarambalam, including Vallika while the rest, were restored safely in a museum.

Flairs and Glairs, a platform by a student for   the students. We are esteemed youth struggling to carve out our path for our future and we follow a basic mindset Since everyone is not born with allround skills. Joining hands with people who are born to execute it with perfection is the best way to evol ve. Self-Evolution is the need of the hour but, evolving as a community is what we strive for.   The initiative as kickstarted by, Founder - Mr. Shubham Shah with the motive to utilize the skillset and talent of writing has now a team of 10+ people who are actively participating into newer forms of learning and discovering talents among youngsters. We Provide platform and services like Publishing opportunities, Open mics, Workshops, Hands-on training. Operating with Brand Name of Flairs and Glairs (Publication House), we offer the chance of elevating a passionate writer to an esteemed author   With Brand name Teekhe Zasbaaat. We bring to you an opportunity to get accustomed with the Public Speaking and Presenting of Thoughts along with regular challen ges to brush up your inking spirit.   The newest initiative to extend our services we introduced in a new writing Platform- The Glittering Fables and Ink Over Tears.

We Choose to Fly Like A Falcon than to be

a Leg Pulling Crab.

To Know More: Infoline – 7781900870
Mail Us At-
flairsandglairs@gmail.com / info@flairsandglairs.in
Or Visit is at
www.flairsandglairs.com / www.flairsandglairs.in
Social Handles- @flairsandglairs @teekhezasbaaat

www.ingramcontent.com/pod-product-compliance
Lightning Source LLC
Chambersburg PA
CBHW070552160726
48003CB00005B/2005